Dunedin

A mystic journey...

Dominique Weiss

ISBN:0692570756
ISBN-13:978-0692570753

DEDICATION

Thanks to Suzie for all your help and all my family and friends that have inspired and helped me along my way. Special thanks to all the wonderful towns of New England area, a mystical and magical place indeed. Thanks to Sadie for her unyielding patience and smiles that always light my day. Special thanks to my Lighthouse and Compass, for without you both I never would have gotten this far and taken the chance to go this wonderful adventure that dreams are made of...

CONTENTS

ACKNOWLEDGMENTS

Gracious help with:
Book cover by Michelle MacGregor
Editing by Suzi Radosevich

Supporter of Wag N O2 Fur Life
An organization
Dedicated to providing pet oxygen masks
to EMS responders across North America
to help them save
animals lives.

PART 1

THE JOURNEY BEGINS...

The sweet melodic song of a Chipping Sparrow sang notes of love on a beautiful summer day. Trees bounded across the rolling hills as far as the eye could see, and so lush one felt like you could just breathe in the greenery all around you. The clear blue sky encompassed the trees as a backdrop to the frivolity of the birds and butterflies, as they flutter around gracefully in tune with the music of the land. All around you there is beauty and light as if God had blessed this magical land and protected it, keeping it special just for you...

Along the path of adventurous souls comes a place where two points meet in time, where one adventure joins another. Today, two great adventurers meet along the wooded path, destined to create friendships and grand stories of the great times awaiting to be shared upon their journey.

A thin Irish lad wearing a brown tweed vest and matching hat, walked towards a raven-haired womyn dressed in a black hooded cloak and held a carved wooden staff.

"Aye, Hello there, how are you?" Said the Irishman in the brown hat.

"Aye, Hello, most excellent I am, and you?" Said the womyn in the black hooded cloak.

"Aye, as happy as baby laughing in a bowl of bubbles!" The Irishman said grinningly.

"Aye," she said as she smiled, "My name is Aingeal, what's yours?"

"Oh me, my name is Finneas O'Malley, my friends call me Finn! Only my Mum calls me Finneas, usually when she has something important to tell me... so please, please call me Finn!" He said as he stood on a log in the densely wooded forest.

"Ok, Finn, nice to meet you!" Aingeal said.

"Which way are you headed, Aingeal, my friend?"

"This way and that! Here and there!" Aingeal said,

As she flipped her hood back off her head, and flung the opening of her cape around to the side of her.

"Right you are, why limit yourself when the fun is out there!" Finn said, as he gracefully gestured out to the forest.

"It's the gypsy life and adventure for me!" Aingeal said.

"Aye, Life is what you make it!" Finn said, smiling.

"So whom is this man called Finn, who stands on the path before me?" Aingeal says, as she exposes the grand sword on her hip.

Finn stands up on a log and swings around a tree and said,

"I am an Irish Lad, Salt of the Earth, Heart of Gold and strong as an ox to stand up with you. I'm a thin lad, but don't let that fool ya, I can box with the best of them or run away clean... You know you've got to use your head and pick your battles, so you can live for another day!" Finn said, as he pointed to his head and walked back and forth on top of the log.

"I see, a good Irishman, strong and true." Aingeal said as she adjusted her satchel.

"Aye, and where is the lovely Aingeal from?" Finn said inquisitively.

"Aye, that is a question that has many answers. I am from everywhere, and nowhere, I have lived in so many places and been to so many lands and each one has been a jewel, no matter where I roam, it seems I am still trying to find home." Aingeal said as she stood up and gazed deep into the forest with her staff in her hand.

"Each place has its fond memories of how I have lived and wonderful people I have met and loved along the way. Some people stay true to me to this day as family would in every way! When people say they are from this town, their whole life long, they have pride and family that make them strong. I have friends in this town and that, and that makes me strong, kind of like that. Some have chosen me to become a part of their family, and that is forever special to me, for no matter how long I roam, there will always be places I can call a home!" Aingeal said joyfully, as she looked at Finn and eased her cloak behind her.

"Aye, I too am a traveling man. I take after my Grandpa! The greatest man I have ever known!" Finn said, with a smile.

"He was a true gentleman, a man among men. He lived his life honestly, and was respected wherever he went."

"Always look your best, he said, no matter where you are... Take pride in yourself and others will too!"

"Aye, he was a great man...bless his heart...Good words to live by..." Finn said, with his hat in his hand.

"So, to follow the great words of my Grandfather, I always wear nice pressed pants, shirt and vest and an Irish cap upon my head. A lovely pocket watch to tell the time, a smile on my face and my shoes are shined!" Finn said, expressively as he whirled around on the log.

"Well Finn, a dapper man, you are, sounds like your Grandfather was a great man. It would have been an honor and a treasure to have met him. Perhaps, like your Grandfather, we both have a wee bit of gypsy blood running through our veins." Aingeal said as she gazed out into the forest.

"Aye, I know what you mean! There is so much to see, so much of the world to experience, people to meet and places to go! Finn said, as he jumped off the log.

"Like I always say, you don't know until you go!" Aingeal said as she smiled.

"Aye, ...would you like to hear a story?" Finn said with his hands in his vest pockets.

"That I would!" Aingeal said, sitting down upon the log and getting comfortable. The forest around them also seemed at ease as she sat to listen to his grand tale.

"Aye, all righty then!" clearing his throat and sitting with one hand on his knee. He leaned in a bit, poised to tell his tale. The forest around them got quiet as if it too were listening, eager to hear the stories of the Irish lad. The daylight chased the sun, and Aingeal gathered some wood around where they sat and started a fire. The wood crackling in the fire echoed into the forest. A calmness and ease surrounded them as Finn began to tell his tale.

Part 2

The Land of Dunedin

"Aye, let me tell you a great story about a wee land that I know... where the Trees are Grand and the Land seasons with snow!" Finn says, stretching his arm way up into the sky.

"Tis a Free Land where wee ones and Faeries frolic. It is a place of Light and Magic, Music and Art. Where the people are free to be... to Think... to Create... all together in a place of Light and Love, a place to call Home." Said Finn.

"Aye, you see, it is our differences that make us special. Here you are celebrated and revered for being you. It is your differences that are your gifts! Your gifts are to be treasured, and by sharing those gifts you inspire others! It is way more fun to share with others, it just makes everything brighter!" Finn said, with his hand on his knee.

"Where is this place?" Aingeal said inquisitively.

"Well, there are Lands like this one all over, you know, you just have to find them... I have been to a few here and there. The one I am going to tell you about is in the Northeastern part of the country. It is a beautiful Land with Trees as tall as the Sky is Grand and the people are one with the land." Finn said, as he stretched his arms out wide and spinning around.

"Aye, the Land... this place, she holds my heart! I feel like a part of me is missing, or rather an empty feeling when I am not near her, so I must always return to the place that holds my heart... the Land, the People, this place, they nurture my soul with Love, with Light!" Finn said happily holding his hands over his heart.

"That sounds like a beautiful, wondrous place! Aingeal said, as she flipped her hair back behind her ear, revealing a heart shaped birthmark on her cheek and a turquoise earring in her ear.

"You see, some people search their whole lives to find home. Some people can't wait to leave home and some people can't wait to get home. Let me tell ya what I have found... Every soldier, every man, every womyn, child, animal or faerie, they all are trying to find home, whether here now or in the afterlife, they all just want to get home... So, if you find that special place in the Light, where you are loved, where your heart is light, where you can breathe, and be aligned with people who lift you up to be a better you, than that is the place to call home... Cherish it, protect it, for that is where you belong... that my friend is home." Finn said, looking towards Aingeal.

"Aye, said Aingeal, you are so right, to find that special place, to be able to breathe, to be held up in the trusting arms of family and friends. To truly just be and create a better world, happily and be loved, that is the key... Love, it's all around us, it is a precious thing..."

Finn leans backwards on the log and puts his hands behind his head and stretched out his legs, and relaxed.

The forest feels at ease and comforting around them. The quiet is subtle and attentive as the fire crackled in front of them, giving depth to the forest.

"All this talk about home, and I haven't told you any of the story yet! Right, would you like a spot of tea? I have a kettle warming on the fire over here... Oh and I think there might even be a cookie or two in that jar over there. You can't have tea without cookies! My friend Aire baked the cookies. She is the best. She bakes these little cakes that are so light and fluffy like... like... air! That's right, air! She has the gift of baking cookies, they put a smile on your face every time! We will probably meet her later, she lives just down the road, a bit." Said Finn.

Finn stirs his tea. "Well now where was I? "

"Oh yea, telling you about ... "

"What's the name of the place, Finn? Aingeal says as she took a bite of her cookie.

"What I didn't tell ya?" Finn said as he scratched his chin.

"Oh well, I thought I told you. Every great land has a great name. This wonderful lands name is Dunedin!" Finn said.

"Dunedin, that is a beautiful name, isn't that where Faeries come from?" Aingeal said as she sipped her tea.

"Well, back in the Times of old, Dunedin was the Scottish Gaelic name for Edinburgh, and there were Faeries and magical creatures everywhere!" Finn said.

"Well where did they go?" Aingeal said, curiously.

"Well I don't really know, but I do know there are still some around here and there, you just have to believe that you will find them... and perhaps you will!" Finn said with a wink.

"All right then, where was I... Oh yea I was telling you about Dunedin!" Finn said.

"Well, you know, come to think about it, it would probably be better if I showed you." Finn said.

"You can't just see this place off the road, it's hidden in the trees, and even I have a hard time finding it sometimes." Said Finn.

It is one of those magical places that you just have to know in your heart where it is and then you will find your way!" Finn said as he scratched his head.

"You see how the bushes go this way and that way, they hide the entrance. There is this archway of bushes... kind of like a tunnel..." Finn said as he scratched his chin.

"It is around here somewhere... you will know it when you see it. It looks like the entrance to a magical land... yet hidden ...The Faeries usually make the entrance beautiful, with pretty white flowers and clovers. They really do a great job of making things look nice those Faeries." Finn said.

"Well help me look for little white flowers and clovers... kind of like that over... there! Finn said all excited!

There to the left was an archway of bushes and vines, with clovers and tiny white flowers in curved lines leading up to the opening in the forest. As soon as they took a step into the archway it was like they stepped into a bubble of light. They were surrounded by light and Aingeal and Finn instantly felt happy and had smiles on their faces. It just felt right, just like Finn said, it is a special magical place.

"See there, now, look at that! I knew we could find it!" Finn said with a smile.

"Isn't it beautiful...? Look what those faeries did with those beautiful tiny white flowers. It is as if they flew down the path weaving to and fro, delicately skimming the ground and magically placing the flowers beautifully on the trail! You don't see that in the city do ya! "Finn said as he smiled.

"I try my best to walk lightly on the path, with all those pretty flowers, but I've got big feet! Finn said as he pointed to his foot.

"I think though that if the forest knows you are trying, it will be a wee bit forgiving and help you along your way!" Finn said.

The bushes and trees were green and arched around them like a tunnel. They had to duck their heads in a couple of places to get through, but it wasn't far.

"Be careful now mind your head, some of the bushes have thorns... one day I came through here, not paying much attention, and a thorn just ripped through my ear, but then one of the Faeries gave me this cool earing ... looks pretty nice, Aye... Luck of the Irish, don't you know!" Finn said as he showed his shiny silver earring.

"Oh yea, that is nice, and shiny too!" Aingeal said smiling.

"Yup, that is a bit of Irish Luck! How else can you get a cool earing from Faerie?" Finn said with a grin.

Finn starts walking down the path with Aingeal. The path is layered with pine needles and leaves giving softness to the curving path through the great green woods.

"It is a bit of a walk, and now mind where you step... watch out for the wee ones, the young trees, they are just starting out and need all the help they can get." Finn said as he pointed to the little tree sprouting up from the ground.

"Oops, just barely missed that one. I will try and be more careful." Aingeal said stepping lightly around the wee tree.

"Oh, aye, and by the way, just so you know, watch out for the roots of the trees too!" Finn said.

"What do you mean?" said Aingeal.

"Well, the Trees roots are like their feet... and you know what it is like when someone steps on your foot... it hurts, well, same thing with the trees roots. So try your best to be respectful, just like you would to your Mum." Finn said as he stepped over a root.

"One doesn't realize sometimes that our steps may affect the greatness of others. It is just a wee tree now, but look at what it may become... a great tree! The smallest gesture can create a positive change, lighting the path for all along the way. It's kind of cool, don't you think..." Aingeal said smiling.

The trees around them seem to stretch out to the heavens, and arch across to one another over the path like the ceiling of a great cathedral. It is beautiful and awe inspiring to be within the arms of greatness.

"Some of these trees have been here for hundreds of years! Maybe even a thousand! That is really a long, long time!" Finn said as he pointed up to the trees.

"These trees have been here longer than your great, great, great, great Grandpa! They have stood here and watched thousands of sunsets and the world evolve. They are like the guardians of the earth. They are all connected from sea to shining sea. They have seen families grow and their family's family grow, and settlers and Indians and the age of Faeries. They are like Time Lords, a benchmark in time, they are the guardians of the land." Finn said as he looked up at the trees in amazement.

"You really admire them, the trees, don't you?" Aingeal said.

"I do, they are something more than anything I can explain. Trees live longer than any other being on this earth, they connect to one another and communicate. Trees are strong, they survive through all weathered storms, protect and help one another like family. Trees bend towards another reaching out to help and to love. They will bend or grow away from bad things as best they can. They comfort one another and can dance with the wind. Trees heal us, unconditionally, in ways so giving, sharing their energy, to help create a new. They are an essential life force of the earth. They are more, and I am very grateful for them." Finn said smiling.

"Aye, truly amazing." Aingeal said. They both stood and gazed around them up into the canopy of trees. The wondrous giants around them stretching into the heavens with green life abound.

"There is something magical about just being still and listening to the forest..." Aingeal said, as she looked up at the trees.

"Aye, it is peaceful, I could stay here for hours." Finn said, taking a deep relaxing breath.

"It is quite Zen..." Aingeal said closing her eyes and breathing slowly and simply listening to the forest.

The two stood there in silence for a while and just listened to the forest. The light energy of the forest surrounded them, and they were both happy and at peace.

Part 3

When is a Tree not a Tree?

After a rest, our two friends continue on their journey. All of a sudden, out of the corner of her eye Aingeal sees a shiny sparkle.

"Did you see that?" Aingeal said pointing over towards where she saw the sparkle.

"See what?" Finn said.

"I dunno, it was a sparkle, do you think it was a faerie?" Aingeal said all excited.

"Oh, where, you are lucky, they are all around us. You know they only let you see them when they want to, they must know that you are good folk, to let you see them. That is pretty special indeed!" Finn said excited.

"It was sparkly, like a little snowflake light!" Aingeal said.

"Aye, they are faster than a hummingbird and brighter than a star, they are truly magical..." Finn said.

"Oh, perhaps they will join us for tea!" Aingeal said smiling.

"It has got to be great being a faerie, flying around, making things look beautiful and look great doing it! What could be better?" Finn said happily.

"Aye, it would be way cool being a faerie!" Aingeal said.

"Those faeries really work hard making things nice for everyone, spreading flowers, and adding quaint little accents everywhere. Perhaps it is Faerie Magic that helps to inspire those like Martha Stewart, and others, a true gift to be proud of! Finn said.

"Aye, there are houses decorated so quaint with flowers and thoughtful accents in New England, that one wonders, if perhaps it was a wee bit of faerie magic that helped make it so beautiful." Aingeal said and smiled.

"Aye, I have heard that Faeries have a sweet tooth, and to show respect, I try to leave a little something sweet out for them, and maybe a wee dram of cider for the wee folk. I try to put it on a tree stump out in the back yard." Finn said.

"How do I know which one?" Aingeal said inquiringly.

"Well, it would be somewhere that looks nice, maybe some pretty flowers growing near, or maybe some clovers and mushrooms. Those faeries can take an ordinary stump and turn it into something beautiful. Faeries just make things better. They love to have fun too, put some faeries and wee folk together and boy you have a party!" Finn said.

"Some of my wee folk friends are great chefs! They do some amazing things with the local produce here that will surely tantalize your taste buds! When you meet them you will just love them!" Finn said excitedly.

"So let's go, we're almost there... I will introduce you to Mother. Well, she is not my Mother by birth, but she is a Mother just the same." Finn said as they walked down the path.

"Now, I have been truly blessed, in my travels, with having met a few Mothers that do consider me apart of the family, and every one of them are Great too!" Finn said with his hand over his heart.

"This one is different...She is a Tree!" Finn said. "That's right, a tree! " Finn said with excitement and reverence.

"How can a tree be your Mum?" Aingeal said.

"Well I don't know how to explain it to you, but I will try!"

"I am not daft, you will understand better when you see her." Finn said.

Finn stopped walking and rubbed his chin, thinking.

"Well listen, and I will try to explain it to you..." Finn said.

Finn stood there for a minute and looked around at the trees, and stroked his chin in contemplation.

"Well, She is the beginning of all things in this land. She is the first One; she is the Greatest Tree ever.

She is beautiful and tall and her trunk is strong and wide. Her branches are long and graceful and reach out to the land." Finn said and stretched his arms out real wide.

"Mother is the center of all things... and it seems when you look at her the other trees grow around her. Her branches appear to hug the other trees in comfort. Her roots stretch way out into the land, reaching out, connecting with the other trees." Finn said.

"That sounds really beautiful." Aingeal said.

Finn pushes some of the bushes off to the side.

"You see right through here... Now look at that, isn't she a beauty!" Finn says with excitement.

They come out of the brush into an open area, and there in front of them was a massive beautiful tree. The tree had a trunk so large it seemed to stretch from here to way over there. The trunk was strong and vast; it held the history of time within it. The way the tree grew it appeared to have a roman style, fluting pillar, growing within the base of the trunk, giving it strength, as it rose upwards into the sky.

Her branches reached out as far as the eye could see, with a beautiful green canopy of leaves gracefully sheltering her. The tree had an air of graciousness and reverence, beauty and love emanating from her.

The tree was simply beautiful.

There was a flurry of activity around her, with Faeries and critters and butterfly's dancing in the air. Everything was light and fun around her, Aingeal and Finn stood there in amazement, excited with big smiles.

"Aye, isn't She magnificent! Now that's a Tree!" Finn said excitedly.

"Oh, and guess what her name is?" Finn asked.

"Treeza!" Finn said smiling.

"Isn't that a great name… for a tree like that?" Finn said.

"How do you know that is her name?" Aingeal said curiously.

"Well she told me! " Finn said.

"Well, I said Hello, and introduced myself all proper like one should when you meet someone, and then I asked her, what her name was and she said, Treeza." Finn said.

"I wasn't expecting an answer, She could have said Diana, Suzi or Bob, but she said Treeza! Isn't that amazing?" Finn said excitedly.

"Wow, that is kind of cool. I guess you just have to be open to really listening, or at least the possibility. Why, if trees can communicate with each other why couldn't they somehow communicate with us?" Aingeal said.

"That is way cool, right! Plus, me not being the sharpest marble in the box, I didn't put the Treeza and Mother thing together for weeks. You know, like Mother Treeza, funny right! I just call her Treeza, fits her nice, and I just start giggling if I call her Mother Treeza, because well, it's hilarious that I didn't think of that... for weeks, I tell ya, just cracks me up." Finn said laughingly.

"That is amazing talking to trees or rather understanding." Aingeal said.

"Well, I think you can talk to just about anything in the light, the hard part is learning how to listen clearly." Finn said.

"Well, I talk to, my friends, animals, trees, it is all the same, they are all living things, all with a voice, and one just has to want to listen. Oh there is a lot of jibber jabber out there, crickets, frogs, rain, but if you can listen through the noise you can hear quiet. The hard part is simply just listening. Not trying to answer, or offer answers through understanding. Monks have been trying to master this for a long time, Faeries can because well, they are just cool like that, and I'm still learning." Finn said.

Finn went over and sat down under one of the trees facing Treeza.

"I think that the trees are all connected, that it is sort of like one big network, like a family." Finn said.

"Look at Treeza, She is in the center, and all the other trees seem to grow around her. Look, really look and they all seem to be facing inward towards her. That is of course if you think a tree has a front and a back, but you turn a Christmas tree around to see its best side don't you? So why wouldn't a tree have a front side to address." Finn said.

Finn sat there and looked up at the trees and pointed up towards them as he showed what he meant.

"See look over there at those branches, it is as if the tree is reaching over to comfort the other tree. That one over there is bending to hold up that one, like family would. A tree will bend away from power lines in the city, why wouldn't they try to get closer to one that they care about." Finn said.

"You are right, I can see that." Aingeal said.

"There is an energy that connects all the trees, well, all things for that matter...but for the trees it is a family network. They say Aspen trees are all connected as if it was one tree. I think after evolving for thousands of years, standing next to another tree for hundreds of years, they would be able to communicate with other trees. A network, a consciousness, a family connected, communicating and perhaps even laughing at us. How could you not laugh at us, they live for hundreds of years, and we are here but only a fraction of that time. What wonderful stories they could tell us if we could only listen and understand." Finn looked up in amazement at the trees and took a bite of a cookie he had saved in his pocket.

"Well, enough of all that, come on I will take you to meet Treeza and then we will go meet my friends and have some fun!" Finn said and stood up and brushed himself off.

"Right then, spiff yourself up a bit, we got to look our best when we meet Treeza. Mind your manners and all that, "yes Mame," and she has been here hundreds of years so show some respect, I think she knows a thing or two. Right then, off we go!" Finn said and they walked up to Treeza.

Finn stands in front of Treeza and she stretches and sways with the wind. Finn clears his throat.

"Hello, Treeza, this is Finn."

"Hello Finn, how are you, lovely to see you today! Said Treeza.

"Wow, I heard that..." Aingeal said softly.

"You are looking lovely today Treeza." Finn said.

"Why thank you, Finn." Treeza said.

"Treeza, this is my friend Aingeal, and we would like to visit in the forest today and meet up with my friends." Finn said.

"Oh, absolutely, go have a good time, stop by later and we can chat. So much to tell you, we have new wee ones growing and I believe they finished the trail over yonder." Treeza said.

"Yes Mame, that would be lovely I look forward to it."

"Well you all have fun and I will talk to you later!" said Treeza, and she sways, stretches her branches and shakes her leaves.

"You see, that wasn't so bad, she is really nice once you get to know her. Her bark is worse than her bite... funny right ... tree... has bark... barking ...well I am here all week." Finn said laughing.

"That was amazing, I actually heard her speaking!" Aingeal said.

"I know, right, it is so naturally cool! Just simple words and phrases, like you can feel and hear the words at the same time." Finn said.

"I know, it is like there is light surrounding us when she talks, so we can understand, it is truly amazing, it's so simple and effortless, clarity. It is way cool!" Aingeal said smiling.

They continue walking along the path into the forest. The trees beautifully blanketed with vibrant colors of green moss upon their trunks, which seem to stretch up to the heavens. This wonderful green canopy of trees, surrounding them with life abound. To be within this wondrous place, is a grace with no comparison. It is truly a gift, to be among these giants, a part of what perhaps God would even call heavenly. Birds sang their melodies near them, escorting the two along their way.

Part 4

Gems on the Road

Our friends were chatting and walking down the road sharing stories and good times, enjoying the beautiful day. There, just a bit ahead of them is a large 5' tall brown porcupine with white tipped quills and a blue baseball cap on his head.

"Hey you see that porcupine over there with the big quills? That is my friend Tom. He is a great bloke. He watches out over Dunedin, kind of like security here. He has been here for a long time and keeps this place safe. He is a pretty good shot too. There are stories, that there was once a predator in the area and he shot out one of his quills a hundred yards and got that predator right in the shoulder! We haven't seen him here since that day. He saved us all with his good eye and quick shot! Good man, that Tom!" Finn said, as they walked closer to Tom.

"Come on now, don't be afraid, he won't hurt you, you are with me." Finn said.

"Well hello Tom, How are you today?"

Tom walked up to them looking around as if something important he is attending to.

"Hello Finn, beautiful morning! It's a busy day, busy day. Checking the parameter, lots to do." Tom said as he looked around busily.

"Tom this is my friend Aingeal." Finn said to Tom.

"Hello, welcome, can't talk long got to check around the area, one of the squirrel families had a break in last night and is missing some of their nuts. Probably just some kids having fun and ate too much after school. All that running around can make you hungry, still got to check things out!" Tom said, with concern in his voice.

"Well, Tom we will let you know if we hear of anything!" Finn said.

"That would be great! Well, I got to go, you have a great day now!" Tom said as he rushed off into the woods.

"Aye, those squirrels, always misplacing their nuts! But boy can they throw a party! Food galore... nut breads, nut butters, jams and jellies, cakes and pie! Oh those squirrels make the best pie you have ever tasted! ... Mmmm pie! We will have to stop by the squirrel's lair later and have some pie. The Best Ever!" Finn said with excitement!

"That sounds really yummy!" Aingeal said, smiling as she rubbed her belly.

"You are lucky that you are here now because it is almost the Summer Solstice! Aye, it is a celebration, for sure! It is the longest day of the year. What better way to celebrate the longest day than with a Ceilidh!" Finn said excited.

"What's a Ceilidh?" Aingeal said curiously.

"Well a Ceilidh is a party with dancing, music and food! People dance a lot to the music and have a great time! You know what else will be there... Pie! I can't wait, oh and maybe Fiona might be there, she's a doll that one, I am kind of sweet on her... and Pie!" Finn said grinningly.

"That sounds great! Why that's just the sort of thing a gal needs, a bit of parting and Pie!" Aingeal said laughingly.

"True that, my friend! Aye, I do believe my tummy is excited in anticipation of joyous tastings and fun!" Finn said as he smiled from ear to ear.

"Right then, off we go... we will go down this path a bit and I will introduce you to my best lads, Shamus and Sadie." Finn said as he walked down the path.

"That will be great to meet your friends." Aingeal said.

"Well Sadie is a girl, but she's not like any girl, she is tougher than nails that one. Why she had a Grizzly charge her at full speed once, and she didn't even flinch. She just stood there and starred down that Grizzly... that Grizzly came up to her stopped, took one look and walked away! Never messed with her again! Let me tell you, I was just a wee bit worried, but not that Sadie, tough as nails... how many people do you know that can stare down a grizzly! Not many, I'm sure of that! " Finn said, excitedly.

"Wow, that's amazing! I sure would have been scared to have a Grizzly charge me like that! She must really be an amazing womyn!" Aingeal said smiling.

"That she is, my friend, that she is..." Finn said.

"She is a real foxy lady that one, slender, long red hair and brown eyes, and a great smile that will light up your day! Wait till you meet her, you will love her, everyone does!" said Finn as they walked down the path.

"Oh my best lad is Shamus! He is a top notch Scotsman! Salt of the earth that one, a gentle soul, oh he is a riot, best lad ever! He's got long curly dark brown hair and beard, strong arms and legs and he's 6'tall! You don't want to mess with that man when he's coming at you, he's built like a Mack Truck, but gentle hearted like a big marshmallow! Best Lad ever!" Finn said smiling.

"It's not far, just down the road a bit, you can see his house from here. See that smoke coming out of the chimney over there? That is Shamus's house. He should be home then, that will be great, and we can stop by and have a lovely cup of tea." Finn said as they walked towards the house.

The house had a rustic look, with brown wooden shingles and a wraparound porch giving it a cozy inviting look about it. There was wood stacked up neatly on the porch to one side of the house. Wind chimes hanging from the porch delightfully played soulful tones as they were gently rocked by the light breeze. There was blues glass bottles scattered on the rail of the porch reflecting the light of the sun.

There was a garden off to the right side of the house and a few chickens roaming around blissfully enjoying the day. A guitar and few rustic wooden chairs woven from grape vines from the vineyard rested on the porch awaiting company to arrive.

"Isn't this just grand!" Finn said as they got closer to the house you can hear the whistle of a kettle blowing. They knock on the door.

"Knock, knock."

"Just a minute I have to get the kettle." Shamus said.

Shamus got the kettle off the old wood burning stove, placed it on a warming stone on a wooden table in the middle of the room and went to open the door. Shamus was a big man with long dark brown hair and big fluffy beard wearing a long brown hooded cloak. He has a sweet demeanor and brown eyes and a soft touch about him like a big cuddly bear.

"Aye Finn, How are you!" Shamus said with a big smile on his face.

"Better than a four leaf clover in a lucky leprechaun's hand! Finn said laughing.

"Aye, it's been a while since I've seen you!" Shamus said, laughing as he grabbed his teacup.

"Shamus this is my friend Aingeal, I'm showing her around a bit." Finn said gesturing to Aingeal.

"Well lucky for you, Finn is quite the card, he is, a true ace of spades!" Shamus said laughing.

"Looks like we just got here in time for a spot of tea!" Finn said as he grabbed a cup.

"Help yourself, there is tea over on the shelf and there might be a few cookies left in the jar on the table, Sadie made them, she will be over later." Shamus said as he grabbed a cookie for himself.

"Aye, good I can't wait to see her!" Finn said, as he grabbed a cookie out of the jar.

"These cookies are great! Thank you Shamus." Aingeal said.

"So have you seen anyone since you've been here?"

"Well we met Tom. Nice fellow." Aingeal said, as she took a bite of a cookie.

"That Tom, good man, keeps this place safe. I will tell you a funny story," shamus laughs, "Don't stand directly behind the man, I heard he was laughing so hard one time, that he accidentally farted, shot a quill right out and almost hit a duck!" Shamus said, light heartedly.

"That must have been some fart!" Finn said grinning.

"Well you know it was right after we had that chili cook-off, can't blame him though, the whole town was a bit gaseous that day, set off a few alarms if you know what I mean!" Shamus said, as they all laughed together.

"Aye, Shamus, I have something for you!" Finn said as he looked around and checked his pockets.

"You do, what is it? I love it when you bring me gifts! This bloke he travels all over and always manages to bring home a tale or trinket for ya!" Shamus said, as he patted Finn on the back with genuine affection.

"Aye, I got it right here in me pocket... here just take a look at that!" Finn says as he handed it to Shamus.

"What is it a spyglass?" Shamus holds up this brass colored foot long cylinder, and looking at it inquisitively.

"No, look through it into the light and turn it... you will see all these colors!" Finn said, excitedly.

"Colors, Oh, yea, that is real nice, look at that, pretty gems and colors. That is Great! What do you call it?" Shamus said, as he held it up to the light.

"They called it a Kaleidoscope! It was invented by a true Scotsman named Brewster, but when the guy told me what the name of it was, it reminded me of Ceilidh, which reminded me of you, so I just had to get it for you!" Finn said all excited.

"Well that's beautiful! Now that's a gem to treasure! See I told you, what a great Lad he is, and a true gent." Shamus said turning it around in his hand. "Now that's a keeper! Thanks, Finn!" Shamus said with a smile on his face.

"I thought you would like it... speaking of Ceilidhs, do you think that we are going to have one this Sunday for the Summer Solstice?" Finn said.

"Oh you betcha we are! I can't wait it should be quite the Ceilidh! Shae and Ciara and the rest of the squirrel clan are making quite the feast and... they are making your favorite!" Shamus said, smiling.

"You mean Blueberry Pie! Oh I am in heaven... those squirrels make the Best...Pie...Ever!" Finn said very excitedly.

"Oh and Myrna and Muriel are barbequing a wonderful roast again and even smoking some chickens... I can't wait." Shamus said, rubbing his belly and smiling.

"I can see that, you're starting to drool." Finn said, looking at Shamus and pointing to the side of his mouth.

Shamus reaches for his mouth. "Very funny Finn!"

In walked Sadie. "What did I miss? You already got Shamus laughing, aye Finn!"

"Hey Sadie, how are you! Come over here and give me a hug! You are looking as lovely as ever!" Finn said smiling, as he walks over to give Sadie a big hug.

"Why thank you Finn, you are looking pretty good yourself! Sadie said, smiling.

"Well, I do try to enhance what comes naturally... for the ladies of course..." Finn said laughing.

"Of course... naturally..." Sadie said, laughing with Shamus and Aingeal.

"Hey Finn, I saw Fiona the other day and she had asked if I had seen you. I told her no, but that I expected you soon because of the Solstice and that I have never known Finn to miss a party!" They all laughed.

Together once again, the friends shared stories of their adventures till way into the evening, enjoying the warmth of a loving home at a fireside table.

Part 5

The Day of the Ceilidh

On the day of the Ceilidh the sun rose across the trees slowly, bringing light and warmth across the land. The birds were chirping, their beautiful songs, delicately dancing on the wings of the wind, bringing joy and happiness to all those who could hear them.

Treeza's leaves rustled in the wind as she stretched out her limbs with the dawn of a new day. An air of excitement weaved through the village as the people arose for the dawn of the Summer Solstice.

"Top of the Morning to Ya!" said Shamus to Sadie, Aingeal and Finn.

"Aye, Good Morning, tis going to be a Grand Day!" Said Finn as he stretched out his arms and yawned.

"I put the kettle on, help yourself, if you want some tea." Shamus said.

"Your couch was quite comfortable last night, thank you Shamus." Sadie said as she rubbed the sleep out of her eyes.

"You're welcome, I love it when you guys come over. We had a lot of fun last night!" Shamus said as he looked around in the kitchen.

"Do you want some tea Sadie, Aingeal?" Shamus said, as he held up the kettle.

"Please, I would love some, thank you." Sadie said as she walked over with her cup.

"That would be lovely! The comfy chair, it kind of hugs you like a big bear. That chair is soft as can be." Aingeal said, as she stretched and yawned.

"I got some fresh beets, turnips and carrots out of the garden, and the chickens let me have a few eggs, not so willingly I might add." Shamus said rubbing his hand.

Finn said as he laughed, "Well, you're taking their eggs ... can you blame them!"

Sadie walked over to the kitchen and said," I got this great recipe from Fiona, she roasts the beets for about an hour in the oven and they taste so good! I have never had anything quite like them, they were the best tasting beats I have ever had!"

"Really!" Shamus said.

"She must have basted them with love..." Aingeal said smiling. "My grandmother always said, when you make something with love, everything just tastes better!"

"My mom said the same thing! It really must be true!" Finn said with a smile.

"Of course, I would love to cook you gents some breakfast, but I'm not promising anything..." Sadie said smiling.

"Yea, as I remember, we had to put out a fire last time you cooked!" Finn said laughing.

"It was just a wee fire, hardly noticeable! The food was good though!" said Sadie.

"Yea, we were starving after putting out the fire!" Shamus said laughing!

"Well, you guys can cook then!" Sadie said, with her hands on her hips and looked at the guys.

"Oh, no, just razzing ya, Sadie, you go on ahead and make some of Fiona's roasted beets... I will just go out and get a pail of water ready!" Shamus said laughing.

"Aye, very funny... very funny...Shamus!" Sadie said, as she shooed him out of the cabin. Shamus runs out laughing.

"I would love to help you make breakfast, let me know what you would like me to do." Aingeal said.

"That would be great, I could use the help, thanks Aingeal!" Sadie said smiling.

"I'm going outside and get some more wood for the fire!" Finn said laughing as he walks out the door.

"That's right, just keep on running! You'll be back!" Sadie said loudly to the guys outside.

A faint voice comes from the other side of the door. "Only because we're starving!" they all laughed.

The warm glow of the fireplace lit the room as Sadie and Aingeal rummaged through the kitchen looking for things to make breakfast. As the daylight crept into the house, it filled their minds with all the wonderful things that this new day of the Solstice would bring.

Sadie put some beets to be roasted in the oven and Aingeal set the table. Shamus walked in from outside with a bundle of wood in his arms.

"Aye, says Shamus, we have a big day ahead of us! We have to gather as many berries as we can for Fiona, gather tables from people in town and set them up for tonight, and I think we will get some lanterns too!"

"Did I hear you mention berries for Fiona? Finn said as he walked into the door. "I will be glad to go and collect a basket of berries. There are those bushes off the south side of the house. They are nice and tasty." Finn said as he rubbed his belly.

"Well, try not to eat them all before we give them to Fiona, she is making something special with those berries!" Shamus said as he gathered some things to take outside.

"The beets are roasting, we have eggs and some bread and jam." Sadie said as she brought the jam to the table.

"Smells good, I can't wait! I am going to go outside and get the wagon ready for the horses and Finn is going to get berries for Fiona." Shamus raised his eyebrows.

"I am just honoring the request of a Lady, and happy that I can oblige her." Finn said as he starts to walk out the door.

"He's funny, honoring the request of a Lady, I should have had him get the eggs from the chickens!" Said Shamus as he rubbed his hand and walked out the door.

The aroma of the beets and fresh baked bread filled the house. Finn walked in with a basket of berries.

"Oh, Sadie, that smells really grand! Puts me right into my happy place... kind of like... pie does!" Finn said smiling.

"Oh there will be plenty of pie tonight!" Sadie said.

Shamus walked into the room with some more wood. "Well, the wagon looks good, horses are ready, and now I'm going to sit right here, put my feet up and finish my tea!" Shamus said as he put his arms up behind his head and leaned back to relax in the big comfy chair.

"This is the life aye, family getting together, enjoying a beautiful day, and the wonderful smells of breakfast cooking up in the kitchen, aye, I'm in heaven!" Shamus said, as he got comfy in the chair.

"I have one more load of wood here, Shamus, where do you want it?" Finn said as he brought some wood in from outside.

"Aye, that's great Finn. Just put it over there on the left side of the stove. That should be enough for a few days, thanks." Shamus said as he sipped some tea.

You can hear the fire crackling in the stove, there was an ease and calmness amongst the friends as they relaxed and pondered the day's events to come.

"Well guys, I think I will start on breakfast. The roasted beets and bread should be just about done." Sadie said as she went into the kitchen and gathered some things to make breakfast.

Shamus stood up and stretched, "I think I will go and get dressed, be back in a minute." He said.

"Sadie, do you think one basket of berries is enough for Fiona? I tried to gather the best berries I could find." Finn said.

"I think that will be plenty, Finn, and I think that she will love knowing that you picked them." Sadie said, as she cooked breakfast.

"It is for Fiona, she should have the best berries, and I just wanted to make sure there was enough, that's all." Finn said, as he looked at the berries in the basket.

Shamus walked into the room freshly dressed.

"Aye, what's that you are wearing?" Finn said.

"What, this?" Shamus said.

"Yes, that!" Finn said, shaking his head.

"Don't be daft, that's my kilt!" Shamus said.

"A Kilt!" Finn said.

"That's right, a kilt!" said Shamus.

"A kilt, you mean a man skirt!" Finn said.

"A man skirt, are you daft? It's a kilt!" Shamus said.

"Man Skirt!" Finn said slowly.

"O common now, It's a kilt! You have seen me wear it hundreds of times!" Shamus said.

"I know... it's a man skirt!" Finn said raising his eyebrows.

"O common now, Scottish men have been wearing kilts in battle, and ceremonies as far back as the 16th century!" Shamus said.

"I know!" Finn said raising his eyebrows.

"Men wear these..." Shamus said.

"Really..." Finn said with expression.

"They do!" Shamus said.

"What, you think that just because you name a skirt with the word "Kill" in it, it becomes more manly!" Finn said jokingly.

"Well, yea, and that Scottish men wear Kilts!" Shamus said.

"So it's tradition then!" Finn said.

"Yes, tradition!" said Shamus.

"I see." Finn said.

"Yes, Kings and Countrymen all over wear the Kilt, and each clan has a different tartan woven in the kilt to identify the clan that they are from." Shamus said.

"Aye, I see." Finn said.

"These Kilts are woven from the blood and tears of Clans of Old, there is true history behind each and every stitch!" Shamus said with emphasis.

"Well then, that's a lovely Man Kilt, you are wearing!" Finn said.

"Kilt!" Shamus said.

"Yes Kilt! Just playing with you Shamus!" Finn and shamus start laughing.

"Aye, when you girls are done discussing which color Kilt to wear, breakfast is ready!" Sadie said, placing breakfast on the table.

"Well I really like the blue one, and see this cross stitch isn't it amazing how they did that..." Shamus said to Finn laughing.

"Oh, that is, really amazing, really..." Finn said looking at Shamus's Kilt and chuckling.

"Come on now, sit down and let's eat!" Sadie said. They all sit down at the table for a grand meal prepared by friends and be shared as family.

"We thank you Lord for all the wonderful gifts and blessings that you have given, we thank the spirits and elementals that guide us and keep us in the Divine Light. Thank you for bringing us all together on this glorious Summer Solstice and Blessing us all with your Divine Love! Amen." Shamus said.

"Amen, let's eat!" Finn and Sadie said together.

"Oh, boy I am hungry! Those beets are so good! The bread is the best! Pass me some of that jam, please." Finn said with a smile.

"Well Sadie, once again you have out done yourself and earned a place in my heart, or rather my stomach!" Shamus said laughing.

"This bread is great! It tastes like English muffins!" Finn said and grabbed another piece.

"I got the bread recipe from Marie up the road a bit! It is really a simple recipe; she usually makes these into rolls. They are so good and she just whips them up like magic! She made the berry jam too, that woman is simply amazing!" Sadie said.

"Well, she definitely has a couple of fans here, this bread and jam is great!" Shamus said happily.

"Aye Finn, maybe Fiona will make you some jam too!" Shamus said.

"I am sure that the berries are for everyone at the Ceilidh, however should there be a personal note of endearment towards me when she finishes making whatever dish she is preparing, it would be greatly appreciated!" Finn said as he put more jam on his bread.

"Right, greatly appreciated..." Shamus said giggling.

"Right you Lads laugh it up... but there is work to be done today, so that we can party at the Ceilidh!" Finn said.

Shamus stood up and said in a deep and laughing voice, "Right, work to be done...and that will be greatly appreciated!" They all laughed.

"All in fun, lad, all in fun!" Shamus said.

"Right then." Shamus stood up and walked over to the kitchen.

"Thank you my dear that was a lovely breakfast! A fond memory to treasure and a happy belly to show!" Shamus said as he rubbed his belly with a smile.

"I think one more cup of tea and then off we go to town!" Shamus remarked, as he grabbed the kettle.

"More tea, Sadie?" Shamus said looking towards Sadie.

"That would be lovely, thank you Shamus." Sadie lifted her cup over to Shamus.

"That really was a grand breakfast, I do believe I will be happy all day!" Finn said with a smile.

"Sadie are you going to sing a few songs this evening? Shamus said.

"I do believe that I just might!" Sadie said.

"Tis a song and a light heart that is good for the soul..." Shamus said as he sipped his tea.

"Aye, I agree, tis the music that lightens us all!" Finn said as he held up his cup.

"Well then lads, off we go for a day of fun and frivolity!" Shamus said laughing.

They all headed out the door to the barn to get the horse and wagon, humming a tune along the way. The barn door was open to one side. The smell of hay and honeysuckle bushes filled the air. The horse nodded her head as if she knew the day's events to come. Shamus petted the horse, stroking her long reddish colored neck and lightly frosted red mane. Red nodded her head and made a neighing sound.

"That's a good girl, there now, Red, we are going to have some fun today... going into town. " Shamus said as he petted the horse.

"She is a beautiful reddish color!" said Sadie.

"Aye, she is a beauty, I got her from my Dad and named her after him!" Shamus said.

"You named your horse Dad?" Finn said.

"Aye, you are a riot, Finn, aren't ya, No, I named her Red, silly, that was my Dad's name, Red." Shamus said.

"What? He could have named his horse Dad!" Finn said as he shrugged his shoulders.

"Red, best man there ever was, a true Irishman, Heart of Gold! He would give you his left arm if you needed it! This horse Red, she too has Heart, strong and smart I think the name fits her well." Shamus said as he petted her.

"Do you want me to put anything into the wagon?" Finn said.

"Well, bring those jugs of water, and there is some cider around the back of the barn, I think we will bring that too!" Shamus said, as he loaded things into the wagon.

"Hey, how about a few chairs too!" Sadie said.

"Aye, that's a great idea!" Shamus said, as they all gathered things and put them in the wagon.

"Well then, looks like we have everything, everyone into the wagon! Finn do you have those special berries of yours!" Shamus asked smiling.

"Thank you for asking, they are nestled in the basket with a few other things!" Finn said, as he got into the wagon.

"Well thank goodness they are safe, wouldn't want to lose those! Shamus said, laughing. They all started to laugh. "Ok Red, let's go into town, we have a grand day ahead of us!"

The cool summer day brought a gentle breeze with the fresh scents of green trees and honeysuckle flowers. The way into town featured a canopy of green trees arching across the road, majestic and awe inspiring, that created a Cathedral setting for giants and kings.

The forest seemed electrified with energy as people gathered together for the evening's festivities. As our friends rode into town they passed by someone on a horse. They smile and wave and the horseman waved back.

Soon they came across another wagon whose riders also smiled and waved. Our friends also waved back to the people passing by.

"You know," said Finn, "I have traveled all across the country from town to town and this town is so very special. People always wave as you pass by."

"That is so true, seems even in the neighboring towns it isn't as prevalent." Shamus said.

"People always rushing here and there, just don't seem to slow down and take the time to greet one another and give a genuine smile and wave hello." Finn said.

"Aye, that's why this place is so special, real genuine people out here." Shamus said.

"Aye, that's for sure." Sadie said.

The three continue on the road into town, chatting and waving to people that pass by. They are happy with anticipation for the evening's festivities, laughing, sharing stories, and rocking in the wooden wagon as they headed into town.

"Aye, do you know where you are going?" Finn asks Shamus.

"What?" asks Shamus.

"Going, do you know?" replies Finn.

"What, me, going where?" asked Shamus.

"Right." said Finn.

"No, we're going straight ahead." Shamus replied.

"Ahead of what?" asked Finn.

"What?" asked Shamus.

"Right." replied Finn.

"No, not right, straight ahead." Said Shamus.

"Oh, right then." Said Finn.

"No, not right, that way." exclaimed Shamus.

"What way?" replied Finn.

"What way? Oh come on now!" said Shamus.

"You, know where you're going?" asked Finn.

"No." said Shamus.

"No?" asked Finn.

"No." replied Shamus.

"Right then..." said Finn.

They were all are quiet and then burst out giggling, as they traveled on down the road.

Our friends got closer into town and stopped at a couple of homes to grab some tables, chairs and lanterns. They put them in the back of the wagon.

There was just a flurry of activity, as they got closer to the center of town. The simple aromatic perplexities of simmering meats roasting, cookies and pie's baking, and all made with love, was meandering through the air.

"Oh do you smell that meat roasting on the fire? Aye, that smells so good! It is making my mouth water!" Shamus said with his nose in the air and a big smile on his face.

"We are going to have some fun tonight! I can almost taste it!" Shamus said, as he rubbed his hands together.

"All the wonderful food it's going to be great!" Sadie said.

"And...Pie!" Finn said with glee.

They drove the cart closer to the center of town where Treeza stood, and most of the festivities took place.

"I think that we will line up all the tables in rows in front of Treeza there, and maybe place a lantern on each table as well. Then any lanterns left over we can hang around the area." Shamus said, motioning towards the different areas.

"Sounds great!" Finn said, as he started to grab tables out of the cart.

"I will grab the lanterns and put them on the tables." Aingeal said.

"Allrighty then, let's set up a party!" Shamus said, happily.

The Ceilidh area started to come alive as our friends began putting tables out. People began filling the tables with cakes, pies and dishes galore. Fresh roasted corn, beautiful salads bounding with vegetables from every garden in the area, adorned the tables with color and vitality. BBQ meats and roasts dripping with juices, and fresh out of the ovens, beckoned to onlookers walking by. Breads bounded in baskets, accompanied by jams and cheeses by their side. The intoxicating aromas lingered in the air enticing people from all around to come and enjoy the Ceilidh.

They walked by some fresh tomato and basil salad, bursting with color. "Oh, I can't wait to try some of those tomatoes! They are absolutely the juiciest and tastiest tomatoes I have ever had! There is something about the earth here that just makes them taste so good!" Sadie said, happily.

"Tomatoes, silly fox, I'm glaring at some of that most delectable hunks of meat just calling my name down at the other end of the table over there!" Shamus said.

"No, no, no, no, turkey leg and pie!" Finn said, looking around.

"I'm going after that roast beast over there! Yum!" Aingeal said excitedly, with hungry eyes.

"Well guy's, I think that everything looks great, perhaps a few more lanterns over there, let's put more firewood stacked up over by the fire pit and we can take a well deserved break!" Shamus said, happily.

Our friends finished up by placing a few more lanterns in the trees and stacking wood. They grabbed some cider and sat down in the cool shade of the trees, relaxing, enjoying the day and the great company of friends.

Part 6

The Ceilidh

There was music and laughter all around, groups of people dancing, playing and celebrating the Solstice. There was an abundance of food and drink with people enjoying the festivities all around.

The band for the main area of the Ceilidh started to set up. There were two guitars, a mandolin, a flute, fiddle, bodhran drum, and a few extra chairs for people to sit in and play.

There were lanterns hanging from the tree limbs above lighting the area beautifully with globes of color. The people were dressed up with fabrics of various colors from all over. There were many people representing their different clans with colored tartans and sashes of The Old World. The tartans had different colors of greens, reds and blues, woven into specific patterns telling stories of Clan history. Each type of stitch, like the barbed wire of the land, held a story of the Clans.

The music and song held the heart of the lands heritage. Each tune played and song sung wailed the blood and tears of the people. Even the dances were choreographed to represent the people of different lands.

Great care went into every stitch and every knot told a story. The art, the music, food and dance, all told stories of the people and ways of the Clans. Every color and every stitch, every twist of every knot, every length of every note, all had meaning, a story of the heart and a healing by being shared.

The band members began to tune their instruments and the people gathered around them. The fiddle player Breizh stood up and addressed the audience.

"Good evening everyone!" The crowd cheered.

"I am so glad that we could all be together tonight to celebrate this wonderful celebration of life... The Summer Solstice!" The crowd cheered. The night seemed electric with the energy of the crowd. Clapping and whistling could be heard all around in anticipation of a great evening to be enjoyed.

"We are going to play a few tunes for you this evening, so if you feel like getting up to dance a few... come on down!" The crowd cheered.

"Well then, me and my band mates will play some Ceilidh tunes for a while, and then we will move over to the fire pit for some all night music, singing, and a hollering good time!" Breizh said.

"All right then, a one, and a two, and... "The band started playing music and the people joined in to dance.

Ceilidh, "dance" music has a different tempo, it is faster and the beat is different for dancing. The people danced Ceilidh style dances enjoying themselves far into the evening.

Our friends were gathered around a table eating and laughing and having a good time. A sultry womyn all dressed in blue, with salt and pepper hair walked up to the table.

"Well hello Fiona, how are you doing?" Sadie said.

"Very well, I see you all are enjoying yourselves, on this fine evening!" Fiona said.

"Would you like to join us?" Finn said.

"That would be lovely." Fiona said.

"So I hear that you and Sadie might sing a song or two this evening." Finn said.

"Why I think we might muster through, I believe we will wait till the band gets over to the fire pit, don't you think Sadie?" Fiona said.

"Sounds good to me." Sadie said.

Fiona's face was softly lit with the glow of the lantern. The background of the trees embraced her and seemed to lift her up weightlessly from her seat.

"Fiona, you are looking very beautiful this evening, the stars seem to reflect in the beauty of your eyes." Finn said.

"Why thank you, Finn, you are looking quite handsome yourself." Fiona said, as she started to get up.

"You will have to pardon me leaving so soon, I have to create a grand dessert with these wonderful berries that someone special gathered for me. Well Finn, perhaps I will see you around later." Fiona said, smiling.

"I look forward to it Fiona." Finn said as he stood up with his hat in his hand.

"Catch you guys in a while" Fiona said as she turned and walked away.

"See ya Fiona!" Said Shamus and Sadie.

"Well that went well, me thinks, perhaps, she likes you." Shamus said to Finn as he smiled.

"I don't know what you mean, my dear friend. We simply agreed to meet later. It would be lovely to see her sing, it's just simple, that's all." Finn said.

"Aye, so that's what they are calling it now, simple." Shamus said, leaning over to Sadie and raising his eyebrows up and down.

"Well I hope that you and Fiona have a "simple" good time later." Shamus said as he chuckled.

"You guys are something else!" Finn said.

"Well as long as we aren't "Simple". Shamus said laughing.

"Hey guys, let's go over to the other side where the games are being played. I saw they had lawn bowling over there." Finn said as he stood up.

"Lawn bowling, I haven't played that in a while. Great game that lawn bowling, they used to call me "One eyed jack" Shamus said.

"The little white ball? ... Why did they call you "One eyed jack?" Finn said.

"Because I always used to close one eye before I pitched and made it closest to the Jack. So they started calling me "One Eyed Jack!" Shamus said smiling.

"Oh that is funny... "One eyed Jack." Finn said.

"Come on lads let's have a game!" Sadie said.

"Sounds like fun!" Aingeal said.

"Well, all right I'm in." Shamus said.

"Me too." Finn said, as he picks up the jack and holds it to his eye. "Well, are you ready, One Eyed Jack?"

"I do believe I am, there, Mr. Finn!" Shamus said, rolling the ball from hand to hand.

Finn places the Jack, or white ball, on the other side of the field and said, "All right there, One Eyed Jack, take your turn and let's see what you got!"

"All right then, move over, and give me some room. I will show you how a true professional plays the game!" Shamus said, as he held the ball to his chest and prepared to throw.

"Hey, don't forget to close your one eye, Mr. Jack!" Finn said jokingly.

"That's One Eyed Jack to you sir!" Shamus said, as he pitched the ball real close to the jack.

"Well then, I think that will do nicely for the first pitch. Let's see what you got, Mr. Finn." Shamus said.

Finn picked up a ball and looked down the field with one eye closed and said, "Well now, let me demonstrate the fine art of Lawn Bowling to ya, it's 33% accuracy, 33% finesse and 33% I'm gonna knock your ball off the lawn...oops kind of like that!" Finn said laughing.

"You boys are a regular riot, let a womyn show you how it's done, we know how to snuggle up to a Jack!" Sadie said, as she pitched the ball and it landed perfectly on the left side of the jack.

"Well then, I guess you are quite the snuggler aren't you!" Shamus said as he chuckled.

"What can I say, it's a girl thing!" Sadie said as she curled her hair around her finger.

"Let's keep this girl power going!" Aingeal said as she pitched the ball.

"That's a great shot Aingeal. You are up, Mr. One eye!" Finn said.

"That's One Eyed Jack, if you please." Shamus said, and picked up another ball.

"My apologies One Eyed Jack, please proceed." Finn said as he motioned his hand toward the green.

"Let me see where was, oh yea, giving you a lesson in bowling techniques!" Shamus said as he pitched the ball close to the jack and knocked Finns ball away.

"Aye, I do believe that was my ball sitting there!" Finn said.

"Apparently not for long." Shamus said to Finn.

"Well then, I being a perfect gentleman will indeed have to return the favor." Finn said.

"Of course." Said Shamus. "Go on then."

Finn pitched the ball but it was just shy. Shamus looked at Finn and said, "Why thank you for being a perfect gentleman!"

"Aye, I love playing with you girls!" Sadie said as she pitched the ball and it curved over to one side past Finn's ball.

"All right, all right, make some room, let me show you how this is done!" Aingeal said as she pitched the ball.

"Nice shot Aingeal!" Finn said.

Finn picked up a ball and handed it to shamus and said, "Perhaps you should open up both eyes this time when you pitch!"

"I only need one eye open to knock you off the green!" Shamus said as he bowled and knocked Finns ball.

"Nice shot Shamus!" Sadie said.

"Why thank you my dear, it was nothing really, just a little finesse!" Shamus laughed and looked at Finn.

Finn picked up a ball and squinted one eye, and bowled the ball onto the green close to the jack.

"Nice, Finn!" Sadie said.

"It is all skill, I learned that trick shot from a friend of mine!" Finn said laughing.

Sadie bowled again and it hooked to the left. Aingeal picked up a ball and pitched it knocking Finn's ball out.

"Well, thank you, let me throw another!" Finn said as he bowled and hooked it to the right.

"Well then, I do believe that, that is definitely my ball closest to the jack!" Shamus said.

"Aye, good game!" Finn said.

"Always a pleasure, my friend, always a pleasure!" Shamus said smiling and shaking Finn's hand.

"Aye, beaten by... a one eyed jack!" They all laughed.

"Aye, boys, I'm thirsty, let's go get some drinks and go check on the band. They should be on break soon." Sadie said.

"What a lovely idea!" Aingeal said.

"Yes, I do believe that I am a bit parched myself." Said Shamus as he cleared his throat.

Our friends walk back towards the band and Shamus grabs a turkey leg off the table. "I think I am a wee bit hungry too!" They all laugh.

"Aye, this turkey leg is great! Plus it comes with a built in handle for carrying, what could be better!" Shamus said.

"One turkey leg for me too and I think I will have some bread and cheese... Love bread and cheese!" Finn said, and grabbed a leg.

"Aye and a leg for me too, Cheers!" Aingeal said, as she waved her turkey leg in the air.

"I'm going for that mushroom and wild rice risotto, it was heavenly, and I think it even had truffles!" Sadie said.

"Me, I just love my meat, there is something so raw and carnivorous, to rip into leg of meat!" Shamus said, passionately.

"One Thanksgiving, we put a blanket down, and had the turkey, mash potatoes and trimmings, right there on the blanket and just ripped into it with our bare hands! It was so much fun, no forks or knives, just hands and teeth, it was the best time!" Shamus said, taking a bite out of his turkey leg.

"Good times, good times!" Shamus said with a smile.

"Wow, that sounds like fun!" Sadie said.

"I think I will have to try something like that sometime!" Aingeal said smiling.

"Oh, it was great, tearing off meat with your hands and then dipping into the mash and gravy! Makes me all hungry and excited thinking about it!" Shamus said grinning happily.

"Aye, and thirsty too, I think we need to go find something to drink." Aingeal said.

"I think I saw some lovely beverages over there by that tent!" Finn said walking, and turned towards Sadie and Shamus and bumped right into Fiona.

"Pardon me ... Oh hello Fiona." Said Finn.

"Well hello Finn." Fiona said.

"We are going to go get a drink would you like to join us?" Finn said to Fiona.

"That would be lovely Finn." Fiona said.

Finn smiled and Shamus looked at Sadie and raised his eyebrows up and down.

Finn and Fiona walked together ahead of the others as they talked and laughed together.

"After we get some cider we will have to stop by where Kacey and the Squirrels are and get some pie!" Shamus said so Finn could hear.

"Blueberry Pie!" Finn said excitedly.

"Fiona, would you like to share a most heavenly piece of pie with me?" Finn said looking at Fiona smiling.

"Yes, yes I would, Finn." Fiona said.

"That's Grand!" Finn said smiling.

They walked over to the tent to get some cider. Finn got a couple of glasses of cider and turned towards Fiona.

"Would you like some cider Fiona?" Finn asked, as he handed a glass to Fiona.

"Why thank you, Finn." Fiona said.

"You are very welcome, Fiona." Finn said smiling.

"I heard an interesting story about this cider." Finn said, as he held his glass up to the light.

"Really, what tall tale have you heard?" Fiona said inquisitively.

"Well, you know this orchard is known all over, for its great cider. It has been in the family for generations and they have taken care of the land and the apple trees for as long as one can remember." Finn said.

"It is the best I have ever tasted." Fiona said, while she sipped some cider.

"Well, there was a time not so long ago, when something very strange happened!"

"Ooh, really, what happened?" Sadie asked.

"Well, all the land in this area, at one time belonged to the people. They were a proud people living in harmony with the land. As time progressed, people changed and the land was split amongst them.

The land that the orchard is on was with one family for years, but it was the old man that truly gave his heart and sweat of his brow to the land. They say he walked the orchards at night, caring for his trees. Some say, he loved the trees so much that he had sap running through his veins. It was his caring and love for the land that made the cider taste so good!" Finn said.

"Aye, that it tis." Shamus said drinking some cider.

"So, just like the people were in harmony with the land so was the old man. When the old man died something really strange happened."

"What?" Fiona asked.

"Well, the family didn't seem to care for the land as much as the old man did, and mysteriously the trees stopped bearing fruit. The land seemed tired and haggard, as if it was missing something. They say, even all the bees went away. They all just disappeared."

"Bees? I don't understand." Fiona said.

"Well, the bees are a very intricate part of the whole process, without the bees, the whole worlds food supply would suffer because they pollinate the trees to bear fruit. No bees no food." Finn said.

"Wow, I had no idea how important the bees are." Fiona said.

"So what did they do?" Fiona said.

"Well, the family and town got together, and helped to pollinate the trees by hand." Finn said.

"Wow, sounds like a lot of work!" Fiona said.

"It is amazing how people can come together to help in a crisis." Sadie said.

"That truly is amazing how they pollinated all those trees by hand." Aingeal said.

"It seemed like the people and the land were one entity. A type of synergy, between the land and the people, where caring and love, was the bond that kept the whole system going. With love and caring for the land, the bees came back and the family has been nurturing the land ever since." Finn said.

"Wow, that's really fascinating, how something so simple can really affect an entire area. How we live, and work together is so very important, thank God, we are so grateful to stay positive within the light. It really makes a difference to believe in the power of love, for all living things." Fiona said.

"That's what makes this land so special, Love, bees and Pie!" Shamus said, walking and talking to the guys.

"Yea Pie!" Aingeal exclaimed.

"I do believe, that the power of love has brought us together on this beautiful day, so that we might share a most heavenly piece of pie!" Finn said.

"Aye, finally! We have reached the land of pie!" Shamus said laughing.

"Fiona, would you like to share a most exquisite taste of heavenly pie with me?" Finn said smiling to Fiona.

"Yes, yes I would, Finn!" Fiona said.

"That's Grand!" Finn said, as they walk over to get a piece of blueberry pie Fiona started humming softly.

"That sounds really beautiful, Fiona." Finn said endearingly.

"Thank you, Finn." Fiona said.

"Are you going to sing tonight?" Finn asked.

"Why, I do believe I might have a song or two, to sing." Fiona said to Finn.

"That would be lovely, I look forward to hear you sing tonight." Finn said.

"I think Sadie and I are going to sing and Iz and Aire, might also sing a few tunes." Fiona said.

"Aye, those two sing like angels! Aire sings those high notes so softly, and Iz brings fullness, and together they sound so amazing!" Finn said.

"I agree, those two have been singing together for a long time. It is an amazing thing when you find a partner that is your compliment; it is a very special relationship that grows and evolves over time." Fiona said.

"Kind of like pie and whipped cream!" Finn said smiling.

"Yea Finn, kind of like that." Sadie said laughing.

As they were getting a piece of pie, they ran into Iz and Aire. Iz has a slender physique with short brown hair in a short dark green tunic type dress. Aire has a more athletic build with short blonde hair in blue pants, white chamois shirt and brown cloak.

"Aye, look who it tis, we were just talking about you guys." Finn said.

"Really, only good things I hope." Aire said.

"Aye, absolutely, looking forward to hearing you guys sing tonight." Finn said, as he took a bite of pie.

"Aye, this is the best blueberry pie ever! You guys have got to have some, it is a slice of heaven...!" Finn said smiling.

The girls got some pie and Finn offered Fiona a bite of pie.

"Oh Finn, that really is good!" Fiona says, catching a crumb to her lips.

"Aye, Finn knows his pie, I must admit, this is pretty good." Shamus said, as he ate the last bit off his plate.

"Well, I do believe that I am a very happy Irishman, good food, great friends, and good times to be had by all! Cheers!" Finn said, toasting, with his cider.

"Cheers!" They all said and raised their glasses.

The full moon rose and engulfed the starlit sky with its magnificence, so beautifully massive it filled the background behind Treeza from branch tip to branch tip, with an orange-yellow glow. The fireflies crisscrossed the night's sky like shooting stars in the love filled air. Our friends sat at a table gazing into the fire, its flames crackling and dancing on the wood creating an air of peacefulness.

"This is Grand! This is truly what life is about, sharing good times with friends on a beautiful night." Finn said.

"Aye, that it tis!" Shamus said relaxing back in his chair.

"It is beautiful out tonight." Sadie said.

"Aye, look at that a shooting star! Everyone make a wish!" Fiona said.

"I have already got my wish." Finn said.

"Really Finn, what is it?" Fiona said looking at Finn.

"Well Lass, I can't really tell you that now, can I, but I am so happy to be here with all of you." Finn said as he smiled and looked at Fiona.

"Aye, Cheers to that!" Shamus said.

"Cheers!" They all said in unison.

As they enjoy the peacefulness of the fire, Sadie looked up over at the tent where the Ceilidh is and said, "Aye, the band should be just about done by now, don't you think?"

"You know how they love to dance at the Ceilidhs, they probably will play a while longer." Shamus said.

"Hey Fiona, how about you and Sadie sing us a song!" Shamus said.

"All right then!" The girls said.

"This is a song about a sailor and his true love and the sea." Fiona said.

The girls begin to sing together in beautiful harmony. Fiona gazes through the fire at Finn, her beautiful voice enchanting him on every note. The song tells the tale of how the sailor is torn between his true love and his love for the sea. How his heart always guides him, and there, is where his true love will always be.

Fiona and Sadie finished the song and everyone clapped and cheered.

"That was really beautiful Fiona." Finn said.

"Why thank you, Finn. " Fiona said.

"You truly make the evening magical!" Finn said, as he gazed into Fiona's eyes.

"Yes, yes I feel that way too." Fiona said, as she looked back towards Finn.

Sadie stood up and said, "Aye, look who finally arrived, it's Breizh, and the band!"

"Whoo, I tell ya, those guys are relentless! They would have kept dancing all night!" Breizh said laughing.

"Aye, can you blame them? You guys make it a lot of fun!" Shamus said.

"Aye, time for rest, a wee drink and a bite of this turkey leg!" Breizh said as she held up the leg with her hand.

They all gathered round the fire eating food and sharing stories. Iz had brought her guitar over and leaned it up against the log. Boo had her mandolin, Ciara had her flute, Shae on guitar, Ferris on the bodhran, Aire and Iz singing along with Fiona and Sadie.

"You guys really made a nice fire! What a great group of people to play with! We are going to have some fun tonight!" Breizh said excitedly.

Finn said, "I have got a shaker egg and Shamus has some spoons!"

"The more the merrier! It's all about having fun playing tunes!" Breizh said happily.

Ferris lead off with a tune and then they all joined in to play. The music filled the air with light, fun and smiles all around as they had a great time playing tunes together!

Finn said, "Play the song that goes faster and faster!"

"Aye, Finn, the Irish Washer Woman!" Breizh said.

"Her fingers will catch fire, playing that fiddle by the end of the tune!" Iz said laughing.

"All righty then... ready, and a one and a two..." Breizh said.

They all joined in to play the tune, it went faster and faster each time through the chorus... until, smoke really did start coming off of Breizh's bow! They all cheered at the end, smiling and laughing, as smoke billowed off of Breizh's bow!

Iz, Aire and the girls sang a few tunes and the group played on, people all around having fun laughing and singing into the night.

Someone out of the crowd yelled, "Play Rattlin Bog!"

"That's a great tune! How about it guys? You can all join in to sing this one!" Breizh said.

"Aye, let's play! You all know the words to this one! Hum if you don't, because it still adds to the notes!" Shamus said smiling.

They all gathered around closer to the fire to sing and play the tune together. The circle of people were lit with smiles and reflections of the fire. The energy was happy and electrified with anticipation and fun.

"The 'Rattlin Bog"

Ho ro the Rattlin Bog, The bog down in the Valley, O!

Ho ro the Rattlin Bog, The bog down in the Valley, O!

Now in that bog there was a tree, A rare tree and a Rattlin Tree!

And the tree, in the bog, And the bog, down in the Valley, O!

Ho ro the Rattlin Bog, The bog down in the Valley, O!

Ho ro the Rattlin Bog, The bog down in the Valley, O!

Now on that tree, there was a branch,

A rare branch and a Rattlin branch!

And the branch on the tree,

And the tree, in the bog,

And the bog, down in the Valley, O!

Ho ro the Rattlin Bog, The bog down in the Valley, O!

Ho ro the Rattlin Bog, The bog down in the Valley, O!

They sang each verse faster and faster as the lines to the song were added. Each time the song started one had to take a deeper breath to make it to the chorus.

A few people were turning blue and dropping off at the end and only the few with big hearts and lungs survived. It was challenging but the crowd loved it, they sang smiling and had light hearts all around. When they finally reached the end of the last verse, some people collapsed to their knees gasping for air. They all cheered and clapped!

"Whew that was a great one!" Breizh said smiling and gasping for air. "Cheers everyone that was great!"

"That was fun!" Finn said smiling real big.

"Yea, that was great!" Shamus said, as he reached for his glass. "I almost didn't think I was going to make it to the end!"

"Tis a song and a light heart that is good for the soul!" Finn exclaimed holding his glass up and cheering the crowd.

"Aye, that it tis!" Aingeal said.

"I love singing that tune! It's almost as good as apple pie!" Sadie said.

"Did someone say Pie?" Finn said grinning. They all started laughing.

They played music and sang all through the night, laughing and having fun. The glow from the fire reached out and wrapped around them like a warm blanket. Treeza basked in the warm glow stretching her limbs out wide comforting them. The forest seemed to sway gently with the breeze in time with the music. The night's sky shimmered with the lights of thousands of stars. There were so many bright stars that it seemed as if one could reach your glass up and drink from the Milky Way.

Iz and the girls sang heart felt songs, truly blessed, as if singing with voices of angels. Their songs uplifting, humbling even the attention of the Heavens. Their sweet melodies a gift from God, and enlightened the heavens gracefully with their beautiful song.

Fiona and Finn talked long into the night, slowly weaving their lives together like a Tartan cloth. They shared stories, smiling, laughing and holding hands throughout the night. The land around them uplifting their dreams as a backdrop of a tales to unfold. The music played around them, swirling and floating on the wind with the notes of love.

Shamus, Sadie and Aingeal told tall tales of their adventures. The many winding roads traveled abound, with tales of storms, mountains and chasing sunsets, the vibrant colors so beautiful, they must have been painted by Angel's .The smiles and laughter resounded around them which created bonding friendships that will last a lifetime.

The sun started to rise up through the trees bringing with it the warm glow of a brand new day. As the light weaved through the forest the trees stretched their limbs to the heavens and smiled. Memories of the good times, during the Summer Solstice, within the Light and canopy of Treeza, in Dunedin, will last forever!

New Adventures Await Them...

Dunedin

References:

Pubcrawlers "The Rattlin Bog Lyrics"

http://www.lyricsmode.com/lyrics/t/the_pubcrawlers/the_rattlin_bog.html.

Brobdingnagian Bards: A Bards Celtic Lyrics Directory

"Bog Down in the Valley"
http://www.thebards.net/music/lyrics/Bog_Down_In_The_Valley.shtml

References:

"The "Rattlin Bog"

Ho ro the Rattlin Bog, The bog down in the Valley, O!

Ho ro the Rattlin Bog, The bog down in the Valley, O!

Now in that bog there was a tree, A rare tree and a Rattlin Tree!

And the tree, in the bog, And the bog, down in the Valley, O!

Ho ro the Rattlin Bog, The bog down in the Valley, O!

Ho ro the Rattlin Bog, The bog down in the Valley, O!

Now on that tree, there was a branch,

A rare branch and a Rattlin branch!

And the branch on the tree, And the tree, in the bog,

And the bog, down in the Valley, O!

Ho ro the Rattlin Bog, The bog down in the Valley, O!

Ho ro the Rattlin Bog, The bog down in the Valley, O!

Dominique Weiss

Now on that branch there was a limb,

A rare limb, and a Rattlin limb!

And the limb on the branch, And the branch on the tree,

And the tree in the bog ,And the bog down in the Valley, O!

Ho ro the Rattlin Bog, The bog down in the Valley, O!

Ho ro the Rattlin Bog, The bog down in the Valley, O!

Now on that limb there was a nest A rare nest and a Rattlin nest!

And the nest on the limb,

And the limb on the branch,

And the branch on the tree,

And the tree in the bog,

And the bog down in the Valley, O!

Ho ro the Rattlin Bog, The bog down in the Valley, O!

Ho ro the Rattlin Bog, The bog down in the Valley, O!

Dunedin

Now in that nest there was a bird A rare bird a Rattlin bird!

And the bird in the nest,

And the nest on the limb,

And the limb on the branch,

And the branch on the tree,

And the tree in the bog,

And the bog down in the Valley, O!

Ho ro the Rattlin Bog, The bog down in the Valley, O!

Ho ro the Rattlin Bog, The bog down in the Valley, O!

Now on that bird there was a feather,

A rare feather and a Rattlin feather!

And the feather on the bird,

And the bird in the nest,

And the nest on the limb,

And the limb on the branch,

And the branch on the tree,

And the tree in the bog,

And the bog down in the Valley, O!

Ho ro the Rattlin Bog, The bog down in the Valley, O!

Ho ro the Rattlin Bog, The bog down in the Valley, O!

Now on that feather there was a flea, A rare flea, a Rattlin flea!

And the flea on the feather,

And the feather on the bird,

And the bird in the nest,

And the nest on the limb,

And the limb on the branch,

And the branch on the tree,

And the tree in the bog,

And the bog down in the Valley, O!

Ho ro the Rattlin Bog, The bog down in the Valley, O!

Ho ro the Rattlin Bog, The bog down in the Valley, O!

Key D

Verse/chorus

D G D A7

D G D A7-D

ABOUT THE AUTHOR

Dominique Weiss's adventures took her cross country in an RV to New England. There she met all the wonderful people and neighboring towns of the area. She settled in a quaint town of Sterling, Massachusetts, where this book was created. The stellar people of Sterling, Lancaster, and West Boylston, Massachusetts, and New Hampshire were good-hearted and stout. Their strength and kindness truly genuine. The adventures through the woods of the DCR and neighboring areas were a special gem that will be treasured forever.